# MAN IN THE DRAGON SCALE COWL

## A FANTASY STORY

JONATHAN EVAN HUDSON

# MAN IN THE DRAGON SCALE COWL

# CHAPTER
# ONE

The man wore the cowl and cloak like he had something worth hiding, but he was in a jail cell as dank as a pot hole during a downpour, so maybe he was, maybe not. It was a dragon scale cowl and cloak, both as notoriously pale blue as the sky itself, or more so, like the sky dragons that ruled those ever clear skies. Skies no clouds ever dared taint white, but everyone knew no serpent would let the man live if they saw him in dragon scale.

If.

No window let a stray passerbier see inside the cell. Nearest light was from a bronze lantern filling the air with the smell of lemongrass lantern and it hung far down the opposite end of the narrow hallway. A hallway that arched around the cell like a capital L for Loser so the cell faced away from that one and only entry way and light.

And the door of the only entry was shut with solid sturdy

oak and locked tight with the strongest steel. The way he sat his tall broad shoulders up, held his chest of brawn out and steady, you'd think it made the man in the dragon scale cowl proud.

The air was staler than the bread in his hand, but none of the telltale stinks of piss and worse fouled the air. For now.

Not even a hint of alcohol ... fresh from the bottle—or the gut. There was plenty of that in the other cells along the hallway. All empty, except for the stray rat.

The stone walls should of echoed every scratch and bang from rodents and bugs inside them and out, and the cracked stone should of carried every whine and yelp from the horses in the stable nearby.

But no.

It was silent. More silent than a stray crooked shanty of an inn the instant the sheriff slogs in.

You'd think it was the eye of another typhoon. But no typhoon had ever hit this part of the world. Even a thunderstorm was scarce nowadays. Just the occasional downpour from a clear blue sky. If the inhabitants were lucky and they ain't that lucky that often.

If only the salt on his lips was from the sea. A scruffy black beard of short stubble was visible under the cowl, but the streaks of pale blue in it ... not gray – pale blue.

Yes. Pale blue.

Too much like the sky itself.

So the beard, it covered more than it explained, and it was clear the man in the dragon scale cowl preferred it that way.

No other man had blue streaks in their beards. None who lived to tell of it.

None whose corpses were intact.

Identifiable.

Only rumors of such had been heard in this town of Graysherd. Even fewer of such corpses had been seen in the whole realm of the Divine Kingdom, but whether Graysherd was part of the Divine Kingdom, the residents might say no, but the Goddess Empress might say yes – but her troops don't ever bother crossing those distant mountains known as the Storm Breakers, so none of them need to know, and the residents of Graysherd don't see a need to let 'em know.

The man in the dragon scale cowl and cloak didn't mind. It was none of his business. In fact, it was more peaceful in here, sitting on a small bench that hung off the crumbling wall like a simple ledge, rather than sitting on some stool in the lone tavern where the locals drank themselves rowdy while clanging away on their mugs.

Cheaper too.

A penny for a night wasn't bad. Not unlike some towns he knew better long ago, and plenty he stopped over since. His pouch was still on him, thank the Light, so was his purse of pennies, but it had gotten far too light to spare a single penny for the time being.

It was a relief to know it wouldn't be lighter after tonight. It would be lighter sooner enough without the help of hidden sticky fingers either.

And one of the reasons his dragon scale slacks, shirt, and jerkin were hidden by the cowl and cloak. His pants were as dark blue as the blizzard basilisk he slew and pelted for it. He tucked them snug under his serpent suede boots. His shirt was white as the snow serpent he skinned for it, but his jerkin was as pale blue as his cowl and made from the limb of his arch-nemesis, the one and only notorious dragon known as the Jacculus Jack.

Yes, that Jacculus Jack, the very same sky dragon that razed a whole human realm to ruin in single day, but those memories were best left in the past. Dwelling on them was left for restless nights, not now, when a man needed to be strong and ready for the trouble coming this way.

Yet not a single weapon seemed be to on him. He seemed to prefer it that way. He had enough experience to know and live by the truism of ally today, enemy tomorrow ...

If not enemy today, archnemesis tonight.

The Jaculus Jack would die – and the man in the cowl and cloak would be the one to do it ... even if the Goddess Empress herself would never waste her precious imperial troops on such a vain and impossible endeavor.

For now, he dare not even think his name or too much of his past. The clunk clunk clunk of cowhide boots, like a count-down to a race, a high stakes race where every bit of effort must go into posing for the crowd ...

Someone was slogging down the hall, just like the man knew would happen.

The real trick soon enough will be to avoid getting a nick-name that could be used as a substitute for a curse rather than a title like "man in the dragon scale cowl" which couldn't be used for a curse.

The ever-so-slight huff huff huff wheezing at every step ... it was a someone stout from a strong love of steak and ale. The smell of both in the air, so slight yet so sudden, only confirmed it. The cost of such steaks suggested a man who could also afford the services of those who could inflict curses that needed a given name, a name received firsthand ...

Most of the time.

Yet the hackles of man in the cowl and cloak raised sky high. Not all fat men were as weak as they appeared. Troll blood ran deeper in more men than people expected and it didn't make all of them dumb or stink like an outhouse.

The shadows within the dim light beyond the cell ... the someone appeared in front of the cell.

A someone he never wanted to see again.

# CHAPTER
# TWO

No ... it couldn't be that someone.

The narrow space beyond the cell shouldn't of fit that fat other someone. Nor would that other someone humor such dim light befitting only an outhouse or stray sinkhole. Nor would he clean a jail of unpleasantness just for the man in the dragon scale cowl.

This ledge for a seat was too comfortable too, but that only made it all too easy to forget how the chains holding the ledge up would squeak or clatter from the slightest shift, and silence would be what would give the man in the dragon scale cowl an advantage.

Just like how that other someone cursed his own name so that he'd know who said it, and meant him, whether out loud or in mind, all to track potential enemies and allies. No telling what even thinking that other someone's name would give away.

The same reason the man in the dragon scale cowl refused to think of his own given name. That curse, similar to that other someone, but placed on the man with a dragon scale cowl, a curse with far worse consequences, nameless was good for now. Any given name, even a nickname that was too close to a given name, it could trigger the curse.

The man in the dragon scale cowl knew that dying echo of this fat man's walk … and the walk wasn't the same as that other someone.

The bars of the cell weren't so fat that they blocked much of the sight beyond them. The man in the cowl would not mistake the fat man for the other someone, no, but … the man in the cowl was relieved he still had hidden all his dragon scale clothing under his cowl and cloak – and did not accept any food from this town.

An empty stomach and its aches were better than certain other … troubles.

Back when Jacculus Jack blacked out the sky, had razed down the town in an instant with his endless massive speared scales that shot down like a downpour from an thunderstorm … how this someone survived too.

Impossible.

Out of that hell of burning smoke from the speared scales impact with the ground, ashing everything around that wasn't crushed, and the smaller speared scales raining down on a deadly hailstorm, everything … everyone …

No.

Not now.

The mere hint of the memory made this peaceful cell seemed like noon in a lovely beach.

A beach that now no longer existed except in one man's memories.

Maybe two.

But the man in the dragon scale cowl made a point not to show a hint of disturbance. Not even shift on his bench. He had a clean cell. A cubby hole cleaner than most of the inn's rooms even. So the man in the dragon scale cowl knew something odd was going on.

His weapons were ready but still unseen. Unnoticed.

Yet ... it had to be a different fat man standing before the cell. The fat man was in perfectly fitted pants and jacket, not the usual baggy junk posturing as snazzy flim-flam. The fat man's clothing had the sleek shiny white look that only came from the rarest of rare lycan pelts – a snow vixen pelt.

It proclaimed his wealth as much as the silver cowboy hat crowning his bald head and his massive silver longhorn buckle.

Beside the fat man loomed two guards. A pair of burly wolf lycan.

They towered over the fat man, but it was clear who was really in charge by their reluctance to get too close to the fat man. These wolfmen were only demonstrating how they'd would loom terribly over the man in the cowl and cloak.

The man in the cowl knew better than to start a pissing match here, so he continued to sit calmly on the bench.

Act bored, more or less.

The wolfmen had already transformed their dark fur into solid armor and extended their claws into full length razor blades, so they had no clear and simple way of upping their attempt at intimation without stepping on the fat man's clear and certain authority over them.

The man in the dragon scale cowl could appreciate how, all in all, their armored fur and bladed claws were worthy of the best of the best plate armored knights.

In fact, they were like wolf-themed knights. Their movement had been and was still utterly silent. Better than plate armored knights clanked louder than thunderstorms. No human knight in plate armor could manage to approach so silently.

Not without the help of a witch's hexcraft.

It was a feat only experts in the lycan martial art of Razorine could accomplish. The man in the dragon scale cowl knew he better be careful.

Serpents used such creatures as sword fodder for good reason.

Their black collars were clear bulges on their thick necks. Both collars had a jet gemstone that seemed have a blacker than black mist swirling inside. So not a gemstone. Worse. Far worse. The mist clearly rigged and bound the collar to more than their neck.

Abyssmal stone. Holding the Great and Terrible Darkness itself within it.

So the wolfmen were slaved for life and beyond to the fat man.

Not unexpected.

The wolfmen finally realized the man in the dragon scale cowl would neither be intimidated or foolish enough to bother taking up their challenge, and they backed down.

Next up, something far worse ...

# CHAPTER
# THREE

Zetra just *loathed* how dank and dim this jail was. It reminded her of the punishment box master still forced her into just last night. The hollow echo of cracked stone walls ...

She wanted to shiver but knew better, that she knew bugs unspeakable crawled within them, how many times had such bugs crawled all over her and she couldn't do a thing since in the punishment box, of course, her limbs were shackled tight. Shackled with the blackest of iron like the bars of these now empty cells, and oh my, did such black iron burn her so, her complexion was only recently back to a deliciously peach without the deep red rashes from the shackles.

And here, the smell of unwashed unkept human was still quite strong in them. Very recent.

The smell of deathly fear in them. Also very recent.

The hallway was as tight as her top but without the cozy

stretch the finely knitted fabric had. The top was a cropped high neck with a wide slit down the middle for obvious reasons. If she could distract her target with lust, she could do more than read his mind, she might render him her slave, as much as she was a slave due to this collar rigged to her neck, but the collar of her top was high and closed, and hid the rigged collar and its shame.

The floor was smooth and steady, just like her strut to get into that confident feel she would soon need. The sweaty human smell of her fat master ahead and his horrible love of roasted cattle. She wouldn't mind some cattle meat if it were raw and bloody, but ...

Such pleasures were denied to her.

Even to her brothers Claw and Fang, his devoted bodyguards.

She didn't have a given name to work with, and the phrase "man in the dragonscale cowl" was near worthless for the telepathic magic so common to her kind, and only reminded her how weak she really was.

How foolish she had been to reveal her heart to that fat man who raised them so long ago. Back when Zetra and her brothers had a different form. Back when they were four footed cubs. Her brothers wolves. She a fox.

Lucky for her, and unlike her brothers, she had two forms instead of one, and one was furlessly similar to the fat man's kind of young beautiful woman, but without the natural shyness, so her short skirt didn't make her blush like it would a human, even if it was a bit embarrassing to strut along without fur over her body, but these heels were so fun to wear, and they weren't far different than her two feet gone paw in her other form, a form more similar to her brothers, but as a vixen more lovely than this human form.

But master insisted she not wash for her natural smell, if only she could scent why.

More importantly, the smell of the target at the end of the hallway, the smell of a human treated well in a jail cell and a rare smell indeed. Why would her master treat him so well?

It was obvious the latest trouble in town ... and out ... the master wanted that man to solve it and not be prepared for the usual backstab such man received after a job well done, no, there was something more going on. The smell of serpent came from the man, but not living serpent, and the very thought froze her blood, made her step a little more uneasy.

That smell ... if it was what she scented ... no ... dealing with such a man ... dangerous. The backlash from serpents would ... her foolish tween dream of serving serpentkind and becoming a starlet among them ...

No.

It had been long crushed in the cruelest way by her master, and reduced her from a pet daughter to mere a beautiful trophy to show off and mindread at just the right times and his business ... she did know more of it than she let on, far more than their fat master ever suspected, and one day ... maybe ...

Forget serving those serpents. She wanted to make her own way without them but this collar ... her shame ... patience. Her brothers would protect her the best they could but ... they still cling to the foolish dream of serving the Great Darkness and she ... didn't.

Not any more.

Master's business dealings and the minds of his "partners" showed her far more interesting and fun things to seek in this world.

And maybe ... that man ahead ... as her fat master would say, if she played her cards right ...

But first she must try to break him. A little sly show of sexy should be enough to crush his mind without him realizing it.

Until it was too late.

But if he survived ... and her fat master ... quite the gamble

But it was time to be a gambling woman.

# CHAPTER
# FOUR

The man in the cowl was thankful the place was so dim.

The lemongrass lantern was more than bright enough, but its stink wasn't strong enough to chase away this next bloodsucker. A guy could normally tolerate some lemongrass in the air in exchange for less night nippers buzzing his ear and nipping his limbs.

Just like how lemonade without the sugar was a nice memory and reminder to appreciate the better things in life when they're around.

But this next thing was best enjoyed from a distance.

And memories were best not remembered in case of mindreading.

So the man in the cowl refused to fidget.

He had plenty of practice over the years. Putting it to good use again wasn't hard at first if he was prepared, but it always got harder the longer he needed not to fidget. Not thinking of memories another skill hard to pick up and put to practice.

Yet he mustn't move. Even in the slightest. A single move would make the ledge that hung off the wall creak and ruin this critical moment. Lowering him in the next bizarre game of status nonsense, but loss these games and the final trouble would be all that much harder to waltz through.

His gut already ached for the wrong reason. Like summer butterflies were swarming in there.

If only butterflies really were swarming in there. Rumor had it a certain serpent princess used beautiful but deadly butterfly magic and that was something a guy could be curious about.

But right now, no amount of dragon scale clothing could truly protect him. Only help.

But only a little.

His mind had to be as clear as the lake back at – no! Let bad memories rest like the dead should.

He'd stay as calm, clear as the sea. The sea that had been only a day's stroll away during the dog days of summer back then. Back then, chicken scratch over a stray rock meant danger of a certain kind the innocent never thought of, so the chicken scratch all over cell walls now started to make sense.

For the wrong reason.

A whiff of the slightest, most mildest of hint of mint and vanilla ... it only made his stomach ache for more wrong reasons. His mouth watered for a breakfast he missed a few days in a row by now. Another reason not to open his mouth.

Yet.

Best avoid food for awhile. No telling if it's cursed or poisoned. Despite his brawn, he was now leaner but meaner than usual. Missing one too many meals was the norm for a good long awhile now. His gut could take it. His body could too. Both took worse.

Far worse.

They had for awhile. Built plenty of character, like his old man bragged about. Good thing the man in the dragon scale cowl didn't have any alcohol in weeks, because the source of the fat man's pelts slipped out behind him ...

A snow vixen.

Like alcohol for the eyes and groin, she was, so no doubt blood of the high elves ran strong through her veins. The Great Darkness, historians claimed, captured more than enough elves to breed their women into darklings and demons, and this darkling was in her elven form except, of course, she had her breed's white fox tail, and that tail was curled around legs that were a drool worthy peach desert for the eyes and loins.

She was perking up those fox ears, ears poking out from lush blond hair that went straight down her back and suggestively over that most ample chest of hers.

And she wore a getup befitting a lustful vixen.

She wore a high neck bra top with an stylishly upright collar hugging her slim neck. It all was as blue as her pale blue eyes. The top's finely knit cotton was stretched as tight and flexible as her morals, or at least that's what that haughty pout on her baby face seemed to suggest, and a slyly placed slit down the middle that showed plenty of cleavage that the man in the dragon scale cowl had to fight his eyes not to glance too long at.

His obvious restrain turned her haughty pout into a pouty smile of victory.

A smile that sent the wolfmen scowling silently in double defeat.

And the fat man was satisfied enough to shift his bulk up higher.

Her slow strut toward the jail cell emphasized the length of her skirt was shorter than the distance between the bars of this very jail cell and how the skirt was tighter than the position the man in the dragon scale cowl was currently in, and, to add insult to injury, the notches up the sides went up to the skirt's low hanging waist band and revealed she wore nothing underneath, as if hinting he had no hope either.

Her sandals were also stiletto high heels. Daggers at a pinch from the looks of them, since its blue suede sleeved only the bridges of her foot.

Easy to slip off at a moment's notice.

As he had learned from hard experience.

And this vixen had nails, all long, trim, and the sleek gleam of bright poison pink. With what looked like a razor sharp, snow white edge. Yet her slim hands and feet couldn't hold against serious brute strength, no matter how razor sharp her claws might be.

If they weren't poisoned.

A big if.

A big load of trouble she was. Killing women was against his code, the Code of True Men, and it was the first step toward a darker path, and the reason a number of darklings were beautiful women that needed killing.

They needed killing by a good women, but he'd found the woman for him.

Yet.

Sparing vixen intent on killing him, not always easy, but doing the right thing often wasn't, and this snow vixen dared strutted right up to the bars and knew she had the advantage and was full ready to take it. Even accounting to her hair and heels, she was slightly taller than the man in the dragon scale cowl and far taller than the fat man who was starting to grimace behind her back now.

Few men liked a women taller than them. Few women like shorter men and the man in the dragon scale cowl was on the shorter side.

Her graceful movement was so elven she might as well start dancing around some trees and bushes and singing like some songbird. It was too elven for a vixen. He had faced vixens before and few were this graceful. She defied the fat man's commanding largess and twisting her slim stomach, emphasized how she was curved *slim* in the right places.

All vixens were curved slim in the right places, and even as it reminded him of not finding the right women for him, the man in the dragon scale cowl didn't respond in any way that playful ploy.

The right women wouldn't humor obeying such a foul fat man.

She huffed haughty and held out her ample chest, all to

emphasized how she was far fatter than the fat man too – but only in the best places.

Like all vixens actually. Least the ones he was unfortunate enough to run into.

To the man in the dragon scale cowl, it only reminded him how the rumors and historians were right.

This snow vixen must be the unexpected result of how lycan were bred from captive elf women and werewolf warriors, which were like massive rapid wolves on two feet, or in their other form, massive hairy men who were always bloodthirsty and berserk.

All snow vixens were breed for the stunningly looks and grace of the legendary elf girls they were bred from. Rumor had it their existence shamed elves so much they hid their women, and their men slaughtered any of these fleabags on sight.

The fat man cleared his throat. No longer intent of being less than the focus of attention.

The snow vixen stiffened ever so slightly. Her show over and she not liking it.

A quiet huff from the fat man ...

Her ears sunk and ... she grew a fur coat from her skin.

It was pure white, trim short, and sheeny gorgeous. She clearly combed and saloned often. Did it so well it was as slick as horse salesman before the sale. She now had a pink-nosed fox snout now on her baby face instead of that lovely human mouth and nose, yet she still managed to smirk wickedly sultry at him with, besides that snout, her all-too-human face.

The vanilla and mint scent gained a musk of fur to it.

Ah. She was the source of the mint and vanilla smell. Rumor had it elves had a natural body odor similar to flowers and herbs if they didn't bath frequently enough but he hadn't run into any elves in his travels yet to confirm it. Other vixens he had run into had washed themselves often and hid their ears under common hats and tails under common loose dresses. But any women could change her scent with the right perfumes.

So all in all, odd choice for a snow vixen.

Her fox ears perked up a moment before she locked eyes on him.

Another ploy.

Yet his heart raced like a cattle stampede headed for a cliff.

Typical human guy reaction to an elf girl, legends had it, they were a class of creature known as sirens but made peace with humanity long ago, yet this snow vixen was no elf girl and in this vixen form, no peace to humanity. She would never be mistaken for an elf girl. Her cute but fox snout and pelt, no, but the wide slit in her high neck top showed how that ample chest of hers was furred up yet ... she still held a dangerous allure, just not nearly as strong as before.

Good. Her first mistake.

No need to fight against a fidget. The man in the dragon scale cowl never cared much for furry girls before. Now other lycan women never got this reaction out of him. Strange. No matter how gorgeously elven their figures were, their inhuman side caused no end of trouble, and they knew his code gave them leeway their men did not have.

It was an odd mistake.

Or maybe the fat man's. It seemed she went furry vixen on his command.

And her eyes still held a crisp intelligence, so she should of known better, if this transformation was really up to her. That wide-eyed intensity of her gaze, and ... her pupils, a hint of fear ... and no, they weren't jaded callous or calculating, like the gaze of the many whores that haunted the taverns and streets in busier towns and cities.

As much as she dressed as a high priced whore ... was she really one?

None of his business. They were enemies right now, and like his old man would say, don't show mercy to your enemy, not till you've won, or if victory ... no.

No if this time.

She was seeking something and he didn't like it, but ... the code did said to help a women in need and lycan knew how to backstab better than human women. It was what they were made for.

The man in the dragon scale cowl knew better than to hint at having that something. Mind readers came in all forms and sizes, and if this one was a witch ... witches could be some of the worse of the lot – and not from looks alone ... but looks often weaken the natural barriers of a man's mind through lust and a women's through jealousy.

She was staring too deep, too long, and he didn't like it.

Not one bit. That hint of innocence ... yes ... that was it. Innocence was what she was hinting at, as much as her getup said otherwise, and plenty of whores knew how to play innocent girlie since their pay depended on it.

The tingle down his spine, that zap of rising hackles – ah, he knew that feel.

This vixen was a witch.

This wasn't the first time a witch tried hid her hideous hexcraft with sultry nonsense. Such creatures were the one of reasons he refused to give his name, let alone think of it, think of too many personal memories, until he could confirm he was safe, and he was rarely truly safe nowadays.

A toss away name could be almost as dangerous ... if he wasn't careful.

But the man in the dragon scale cowl wouldn't bother playing this vixen witch's games.

Witches often had long hair in order to strengthen their hair magic. Her bangs drooped over her chest but also passed her top's collar and the fur stretched her top even more that ... her top's collar opened more naturally and ...

Underneath the top's collar was a blue leather collar rigged deep into her neck, with an Abyssmal stone the likes the man in the cowl never saw before. Bright blue? Including the mist inside.

No doubt about it now. She was slaved for life and beyond to the fat man.

Figures.

She noted his realization, and her ears sank with her foxy tail ... like a naughty puppy caught in the act.

But the purpose of her act ... he wasn't sure yet and he already didn't like it.

# CHAPTER
# FIVE

Without the slightest shift on the bench, not even to let the slightest creak echo out, even the chance to move his eyes and risk losing the pissing gaze contest the moment he won it – the man in the dragon scale cowl doubled checked his impression of his surroundings. Witches were well know to fake a loss only to snatch victory in the end. The key was to pay attention to the surroundings without being distracted from the witch.

The dim light hid the walls well. Too well. No telling what might be hiding in the shadows of all these cracks. More than just rats and bugs but he was ready.

His eyes finally fully adjusted to the dim light.

No doubt now.

The chicken scratch on the walls ... a few crumbles – crumbles that only looked like moldy bread crumbles but were actually stone ... they were stuck in stray holes along the edge of the walls.

They were living stone of a sort. Living stone was harder than bone yet could move smoother and quieter than muscle. Despite being gray stone, it was alive and had the warmth, the sheen, the complexion of life, and when it wasn't the flesh and bone of the stonemen tribes, it was made from the darker techniques of alchemy that required a powerful cauldron and an even more powerful magic user of questionable morals.

But this living stone was ... darkened. As if dead.

Mummified.

And that meant even worse trouble was ahead if his gut was right.

And it usually was.

Another hint – the strong scent of lemongrass. Stronger than such lanterns usually are and towns like this one aren't in the happen of wasting precious lemongrass, especially on prisoners, in fact, they'd be more inclined to skip the lemongrass and leave the prisoners to suffer under the gluttony of night nippers.

But this time it was hiding something. A carefully hidden sniff revealed the slightest nip of iron came from the walls.

Rusty iron.

Or blood and iron.

Plenty could of came from the empty jail cells up the hallway, but jailers didn't keep their bars rusty and keep their jobs long. Rust would weaken the bars if left on too long. Even low grade iron would still be polished frequently, even if it rusted moments afterwards. No telling how much of the iron came off the narrow wall across from his cell, or the wall behind the two wolfmen guards. Their wolf stink overwhelmed any simple way of confirming the truth before he needed to act.

The sweet mint and vanilla stink of the vixen didn't help neither. Just her presence seemed to warm the air, but plenty of vixens tended to either warm or cool the air, whether they wanted to or not.

Especially witches. Good way of detecting a vixen, it was.

Strangely, the vixen then fondled her collar's Abyssmal gem, as dangerous and fragile as that gem was, that was brave stupid or just stupid to risk breaking it. The movement gave him a better view of it, and it looked like a ruby as blue as her eyes, and just as shiny, and as pale blue as the mist swirling inside toward her fingers, which was also strange. The mist shouldn't react to her fingers. The stone looked snug in its heart-shaped buckle of steel, just like the youthful vixen looked snug in her lush gorgeous figure she'd have for life, whether short or long.

The snow vixen finally sighed out loud. "Zee prisoner is–"
SMACK!

The fat man hit the snow vixen's snout so *hard* the sound echoed **smack** *smack* smack and cracked hollow down the narrow stone hallway.

The man in the dragon scale cowl launched himself up.

Landed by the bars.

Hands ready to do what his code said was necessary.

"No Zetra!" the fat man said, "Bad!"

But the sudden chill in the air held him back.

It reminded him of who he was and where he was. The

chill tingled the spine and his hackles so deep, it was no doubt from the vixen's own shock and loss of control of her abilities. Common among vixen with ice magic – and a good way to uncover an ambush they were a part of.

The snow vixen named Zetra sniffed, those pointy fox ears of hers sinking deep and tail even deeper, all so ashamed, but of being punished or from the reminder of being slaved to this pathetic excuse of a man.

"Zorry," Zetra said, "I just – eep!"

Zetra suddenly jolted. Frozen stiff midway. Shocked literally and figuratively in place. Her gag caught, silenced her midway too.

From the collar? That's a new extreme.

But not unexpected.

The fat man fumed. "Enough!"

Now normally, free lycan hunted humans, as the Dark demanded of them, so few humans felt the slightest sympathy for one slaved by a collar, and the man in the dragon scale cowl wasn't among those few.

But the fat man's arms was too far to grab.

Yet.

"Your brothers do behave so well," the fat mans said, "So why can't you, my dear? First impressions mean everything, and you, my dear, left a bad impression. I shall pelt you tonight thoroughly."

Zetra nodded. "Regeneration is not vat it is cut up to be, no?"

Another shock froze her. Stuck her in a even more jagged tormented pose.

Yes, it was brave to wise-crack her master. Stupid too. Stupid brave.

But breathing carefully, the man in the dragon scale cowl noted the vixen's vanilla and mint smell again. It was too ... not strong like a typical whore ... it was pleasingly weak but ... he noticed it too strong for comfort and the reason wasn't how it sent heart heart thunking.

Something else was going on with her. Her previous bravo was too playful, too out of place for a creature in such a position.

Yet ... the man in the dragon scale cowl couldn't help but like her for it.

# CHAPTER
# SIX

The man in the dragon scale cowl stood his full height behind those pathetic iron bars.

Such a pose wouldn't intimidate the bars like it did to plenty of men in his past, but just like those long gone men, these bars wouldn't hold him back for long – if he were foolish enough to strike at them, but he knew better than to give in too much to this next form of temptation.

The dim light worked in his favor, just as the glow white of the vixen's fur coat did, her outfit more modest than the usual lack of garb her brethren were often forbidden outside of times they hid in human forms.

He let the cool dank air cool his temper. It was better if he was a sharp as steel.

His boots were solid on the ground. Flat solid ground.

The smell of lemongrass tempered his anger like that memory of lemonade with sugar from a more innocent time, but this vixen wasn't the kind of innocent lass who made such a innocent silly goof up.

The rust on the bars ... that gleam on the bars, they were polished recently yet already had rust ... then they were low grade iron, but not the worst kind of iron for decent frying pans and he could go for some of his customary scrambled eggs with chucks of fried bacon – after this mess was cleared up but he suspected it was far from cleared up.

His stomach did too. It felt too uneasy to risk a growl of hunger.

Not while this women was suffering at the hands of this wicked fat man.

Not while he couldn't risk cutting the fat man down.

Not yet.

"My dear," the fat man said, "It will be more than a simple pelting."

Zetra whimpered, unfrozen finally, and stepped back, and back. Back beside her wolfmen brothers. Brothers unmoving.

Too unmoving.

Their gaze not on the man in the dragon scale cowl, but unseen by the fat man.

Turning to the man in the dragon scale cowl, the fat man took up much of the small between beyond the cell while he fondled his longhorn cattle buckle on his pants with the kind of pride most fools reserved privately for the flesh blade in their trousers.

He wisely stood well out of reach.

"My apologies for the vixen's rudeness," the fat man said, "I'm known in these parts as Cattlesmith Cal."

The man in the dragon scale cowl recognized this kind of fat man, so he made a point not to nod. Not answer in any way.

Not yet.

Why the man in the dragon scale cowl couldn't help but still yearn to hear that vixen's light nasal accent again, especially its romantic undertone that reminded him of the distant kingdom of Fiona ... and someone ... else ...

Fool.

He knew if Zetra and her brother were freed somehow – a big uncertain how – they'd just run right over to their brethren to serve their Great Darkness under the serpents that had bred them and ruled over them with an iron fang.

In truth, where else could they go? It was none of his business.

They were bred into existence to serve their Great Darkness and their serpent betters, so the man in the cowl sat still, but not tense. Let the fat man known as Cattlesmith Cal go on.

"Bad impressions are always hard to beat," the Cattlesmith Cal said, "But overcoming challenges made me a man rich in land and cattle. You might understand."

Then an obvious hint, hint gesture with those chubby hands tugging his longhorn buckle.

Pale clean and uncallused hands.

But now the man in the dragon scale cowl knew why there were so many cattle grazing the pastured mountainsides outside and well beyond Graysherd. The countless spiked fences criss-crossed the land like some chimera of a zombie all stitched together. The fences barred the way for honest travelers, despite the steep slopes being able trap the cattle far better than any fence.

Any rancher knew cattle hated inclines because they couldn't run on them.

The fat man didn't smell of living cattle either, so the man in the dragon scale cowl didn't respond in word or action.

Yet.

"I see you don't," Cattlesmith Cal said, "It is unfortunate, you don't. With such a pleasant welcome, I expected more *gratitude*."

Zetra looked even more downcast now ... she huddled within herself like a terrified little school girl judged guilty of serious misbehavior by an actual judge. Her brothers were too unmoving too, but their looming had a different tone to it now.

Unseen by the fat man Cal.

Of course, both men knew the lycans' collars ensured their obedience as long as they feared death and its horrifying agonies beyond enough ... never you mind the agony the collar would first inflict. The agony for failing their Great Darkness by being slaved to a human, a lightling, even if that lightlings was as evil as any darkling ... all in all, it was just one more nasty legend a man preferred never having heard.

Cattlesmith Cal snorted. "Why I–"

"Get to the point," the man in the dragon scale cowl said — and nothing more.

"Point?" Cattlesmith Cal said, "Geez whiz, we have a quick one here. Rumors might be true after all. I need some points driven into some nasty serpents. Word has it you're the best man for the job. Unless you bought all that dragon scale off some lesser fool of a fool."

So some serpents were feasting off his precious cattle. Not unusual. Cattle were just bigger safer meals to them, and less likely to lead to a territorial fight, which leads to the next question ...

"Any humans taken?" the man in the dragon scale cowl said.

"Not my concern," Cattlesmith Cal said, "But if you want to know ... some beautiful lass and the lot of lads she had twirled around her pretty fingers. Now I know what you're thinking, hoping to wring a few more pennies from the towns-folk, ha! I like you, but I like my cattle more. I'll pay you well for their heads."

Except humans were such a delicacy to serpents they were denied to lesser serpents less they face the wraith of the greater serpents that they "stole" from.

"Whose heads?" the man in the dragon scale cowl said.

The fat man tugged his buckle. "Ha! Good ear. Guess."

"Killing men for coin," the man in the dragon scale cowl said, "I don–"

"Wait wait," Cattlesmith Cal said, "Hear me out first. Those lads did more than push over some of my cattle, they did, they went and stole some, using the serpent as cover, but that dragon can only snatch two away at a time, and I got more than two missing – each time after the first time."

The man in the dragon scale cowl grimaced. "Let the constable–"

"The constable's dead, son," Cattlesmith Cal said, "Killed

by those very lads. Hung and flayed him like a hog, poor man, Light bless his sorry soul. If I didn't have my trusty wolves with me all the time ..."

Not the vixen. She must be a trophy witch. Telepathic magics of course, but little use in a real fight, physical or commercial. Cattlesmith Cal held his longhorn buckle tighter and tighter as he spoke, and instinct ... the man in the dragon scale cowl listened harder to the silent walls.

"Those hoodlums," Cattlesmith Cal said, "They would of overrun the town using that pet serpent of theirs. If it weren't for their serpent, I'd have sent Claw and Fang out to do what's necessary, but against a serpent ... I'm not a wasteful man and that'll be a waste. You get what I'm telling you, son. We're at a stalemate, and I need you to break it in my favor."

"I get," the man in the dragon scale cowl said, "But you're not the type of man that likes owing a favor to anyone."

"That's where you're wrong boy," Cattlesmith Cal said, "You owe a man a favor, that man has an interest your success. Least enough success to get the favor returned."

The man in the dragon scale cowl took the extra moment to note how Cattlesmith Cal was squeezing held his longhorn buckle enough to make his fat hand pale. The dim light didn't hide the sheen of sweat on the fat man's brow and hands or how it was too dank in here to be that sweaty.

The man in the dragon scale cowl savored the pause like a drank of ale before he finally answered.

"Sometimes," the man in the dragon scale cowl said, "Sometimes not."

Cattlesmith Cal jerked his buckle up high this time. What a short temper.

"Course there's exceptions," Cattlesmith Cal said, "Always are, always will be, but son, I'll offer you plenty of coin and a favor in return, a nice big favor, on top of the favor of getting you out of this dank dark place, all you got to do is slay that blasted serpent."

But ... favors have a way of slaving men worse than those lycan under the fat man's control. Lycan who now were quietly yet intently staying in the background, behind Cattlesmith Cal, as if hoping to remain unnoticed and outside the fury of the man in the dragon scale cowl.

A hope no doubt justified by the smell of all the dragon scale on him and the foolish antagonizing by their fat master. The dim light played to their advantage except the vixen was so pure white she practically glowed from the bit of lantern light reaching this dank corner of no where.

That eerie glow, one of the reasons snow vixens were sometimes jokingly called bow fodder. A lycan that glowed in the moonlight, a lycan easy to feather through the heart in the dead of night, the time when lycan were most active, and a heart shot, the best way to cripple a lycan, best way toward an easy kill of a creature that ain't easy to kill due to their regenerating.

An easy target for night serpents too.

And a meal that kept giving for longer than most.

"Maybe I will," the man in the dragon scale cowl said, "Maybe I won't. Describe this serpent."

Cattlesmith Cal squinted beady like a hog whose slop was missing its usual rotted apple.

"Rumor said you'd kill any serpent dead for free," Cattlesmith Cal said, "Just for the sake of killing one more of those scaled bastards. I see the rumors are wrong."

"I was referring to the lads," the man in the dragon scale cowl said, "And the lass."

The fat man snorted like a hog denied his sty. "Didn't sound like it."

"Tell me of this serpent," the man in the dragon scale cowl said, "And I'll decide for myself what to do with the lads and their lass."

"The law will decide their fate, not you," Cattlesmith Cal said, "And it ain't a pretty one, I can tell you that."

To be hung or worse, knowing this region of the world, probably drawn and quartered, whether they earned it or not, and the man in the dragon scale cowl wasn't so sure they were the ones who earned it.

Yet.

At the very least, some serpents had ways to control men. Make them do things they'd never normally do only to feast on them when their use is over and done with.

"Enough about the kids," the man in the dragon scale cowl said, "The serpent. Tell me or else I'll enjoy my quiet stay here a bit longer."

"Not too long" Cattlesmith Cal said, "You see, son, you got caught trespassing on my lands, and it ain't a small trespass neither, it's enough to get you convicted on attempted cattle rustling and that'll carry more than a rest in a jail cell, if you catch my drift."

"It sounds like you know less of this serpent than you care to admit," the man in the dragon scale cowl said, "Or too much."

"Now see here," Cattlesmith Cal said, "I–"

"Two cattle taken at a time," the man in the dragon scale cowl said, "Means it's not a lesser serpent. They're never big enough to rustle more than one at a time and it's unusual they're big enough to even rustle one."

The man in the cowl made a point not to move.

"The town's still standing," the man in the cowl said, "And only two taken at a time means it's not a greatest serpent ... probably."

Fortunate for the town, but unfortanute for the man in the cowl.

"They'd take far more than two cattle at a time," the man in the cowl said, "And leave more than a few scared cattle behind. That leaves a greater serpent and you ain't going to find another man willing to touch its scales for any amount of coin. The risk earning the wraith of their kindred ..."

Or decent woman willing to stay near that man.

"It's enough to get hunted by our own," the man in the cowl said, "I know. I've been hunted myself and know my way 'round that kind of trouble."

But the man refused to think in the slightest of the many times he did so.

Refused to move still.

"But you, without me," the man in the cowl said, "You'll

have a greater serpent on your hands that will get braver and braver and soon enough, the time will come when you won't have a single cattle left. And that's if you're lucky."

That last word made Cattlesmith Cal flinch every so slightly too.

But the fat man didn't interrupt.

"Maybe," the man int he cowl said, "That greater serpent will demand you give it a sacrifice. Monthly. Weekly. Maybe even daily. If it hadn't already done so. And by the time you run out of cattle ..."

Cattlesmith Cal didn't hid his flinch now, but he didn't interrupt neither.

"It won't just be your hind the serpent is after," the man in the cowl said, "I've seen it before. Always ends ugly. How ugly this time will depend on you. Now tell me what you know of this serpent."

Cattlesmith Cal squeezed his longhorn buckle but ... was also cringing, and cringing hard.

Bullseye.

# CHAPTER
# SEVEN

But underneath the vixen's smell of vanilla and mint, the man in the dragon scale cowl detected even more iron and rust than before these visitors arrived. Or blood and rust.

But not from them.

Blood could rust iron and depending on the quality of the iron, do it quick, real quick, like the low grade iron used for these bars. It was low grade enough that it would need a polishing least every few days to stay good and sturdy.

Bad idea for a jail, unless no prisoners tended to stay there long and there were few of them in the first place.

But the man in the dragon scale cowl remained by the bars. Refused to take a step back. The jail was small. Barely enough room to stride. To dodge.

But these bars meant those wolves had little room to strike him back. Stalemate of sorts.

If it was just the lycan that could attack.

Big if and that rust and blood, not good odds.

The fat man Cattlesmith Cal cringed silently and seemed to take the rest of the end of the hallway up. His wolves at his side, slightly behind, but ready for action, and their attention, not necessarily at the man in the cell. Strange.

But the vixen ... just patiently pouty and standing away from the brothers now. She was the furthest away, but posed impatiently but sultry, not on guard at all, and not guarding the way for newcomers or leavers.

For now, the man in the dragon scale cowl decided to rely on his cloak, his clothing, all dragon scale, and more than enough to deter claw or blade, but they would not protect him the sweet enslaving siren calls, or petrifying perfumes, or ghastly gazes of death, so he couldn't be careless, not even risk going too close to the walls behind and risk a least serpent like some rattlesnake or asp slithering out, no, his hands were on his sides, dragon scale gloves on snug and ready to draw his secret weapons from thin air any moment.

Zetra only grimaced. Ears cockeyed but silent. Clearly she read his mind but choose not to tattle.

Good.

This Cattlesmith Cal was certainly hiding more than he let on.

This close up ... the iron in this jail already more rust on the bars than it should. The lock too.

Barely visible but his eyes adjusted to the dim light and the glow of the vixen was helping far more than it should, clearly to her own satisfaction, even if it was just well-earned resentment for her masters terrible treatment of her. It was the key to spotting that touch of red against black.

Too red.

Them smell ... sniff. sniff.

It only looked similar to the rust that quickly grows on low quality cast iron pans. The kind of pans that made the best eggs and bacon.

But it was good he hadn't eaten yet. Eat and he'd risk getting a touch sluggish.

And that touch, the difference often between life or death.

If the food wasn't cursed.

Or poisoned.

Big if.

And that smell ... sniff, sniff, it was, a hint of blood iron. Blood iron was to humans like cold iron was to elves and lycan or alicorn was to serpents.

Cattlesmith Cal was hiding something worse than a greater serpent, and–

CREEEAAAAAK.

# CHAPTER
# EIGHT

From the other end of the hallway.

A creak so loud it smothered all the echoes like some demented father heat-struck into smothering his kids.

It was followed by a thick set of clonks from solid boots walking steady down the hallway. The smell of gunsmoke was so strong the man in the dragon scale cowl barely managed not to choke, but it was like his breath was suddenly scorching his insides.

The wolves Claw and Fang behind Cattlesmith Cal crouched defensively. Glancing down the hallway, Zetra was shocked wide-eyed terrified and silently whimpering. She even fondled her collar under her top's collar and gulped far too loud and wet.

Cattlesmith Cal glared at Zetra. Her brothers too?

Stiffly, Zetra settled in beside Cattlesmith Cal. In a defensive lycan crouch, ready. Her hands transformed into more powerful paws with bigger, more razor claws. Quite similar to her pawed feet before.

Apparently this Cal came before his women and the man in the dragon scale cowl didn't like it.

Killing women was against his code, the Code of True Men, and it was the first step toward a darker path, and the reason a number of darklings were beautiful women that needed killing.

They needed killing by a good women. And the man in the dragon scale cowl hadn't found a women for him.

Yet.

But he was looking. His old man did say he found ma in the most unexpected of places but

# CHAPTER
# NINE

Zetra did her best to fake baring her fangs in defensive excitement upon mindreading the last thought of the prisoner.

She crouched ready to prove she could fight worth a damn, and not just to protect this despicable Cal that, Zetra had read enough books, before Cal had slaved her for ... but she read plenty of adventures and romances. Plenty of the Code of True Men.

How most vixens tried and failed to take advantage of such men but what if ...

She didn't know much of his likes or dislikes. Didn't know much about him at all but he smelled of the righteous rage that her brothers no longer felt for her, not for a long long time, ever since she all but admitted to giving up on serving the Dark one day, and a girl could only hide the scent of her thoughts for so long, because she dreamed of something better.

What ... she wasn't sure, yet, but this prisoner ... if she could convince him to take her with him ... maybe she'd find it.

Her heart pounded louder than this new menace coming down the hallway.

Her slender size gave her more dodging room than either of her massive brothers. The stink of blood and iron came off strong from this newcomer. The blood of the others prisoners that were once stuffed in these cells because of her master. It had to do with his new dealings with something so unsavory he refused to risk letting her mindread for him. Instead, he kept throwing her in her punishment box over and over and over and over.

He never threw her in the punishment box, never had a punishment box back when she was a young and free and he treated her like the daughter he never had, and that was after keeping her as his precious pet cub, during her four-legged fox days, along with her wolf cub brothers.

Boy, was he so surprised when they grew into their two-legged furball forms.

And so excited that ... he even spared the occasional steak for them.

Raw and bloody.

No, not since ... never since she admitted thinking of joining the Dark. Stupid tween dream it was but ... he never was the same.

She was just a lycan slave to him now and she hated it.

But the Dark ... would do even worse to her. Stupid her should of realize it long go but ... but this human prisoner ... was different than all the other. If she could gain his trust ... enough trust ... than maybe ... and Cattlesmith Cal did have a way to remove this horrible collars ... if only ... just play her cards right, as those adventure stories would always says, and your dreams might just come true, as those romance stories always said.

Maybe.

# CHAPTER
# TEN

The man in the dragon scale cowl listened closely to the heavy clonks coming closer and closer to to his cell. How the clonk did echo sharp against the walls and revealed no illusions hid large gaps. No echoes came from within the walls which suggested there weren't any false hallways.

The smell of blood and rust grew thick as thieves at an unguarded bank, one with an broken safe overwhelmed with gold. If he listened hard enough, a thunk-thunk like a steady heartbeat was also ... yes, it was faint, but it was there, getting louder with every clonk, and that meant trouble.

The human ear shouldn't hear any heartbeat but his own.

Except for certain monstrosities.

A slight breeze that should not be here spurred another slow sniff. It was the smell of burnt bacon ... a strange smell for this locale. All it needed was eggs but he knew this was the eating kind of bacon.

His stomach refused to ache from being empty or else it'll stay empty forever.

His hands curled ready to – no. Zetra might be on his side, probably not, but no doubt she could read his mind and he couldn't risk her warning them of his techniques.

No telling if she was the only mindreader here.

Probably not.

The shadows between the gray stones grew darker and darker. A chill worthy of a mountainside blizzard, a rumble silent but stomach shaking greater than a whiff of fresh cayenne pepper chili, and the burn ... a demon.

And not more mundane sort like the wolfmen and their sister vixen.

Speaking of demons, the wolfmen Claw and Fang were far too crouched and prepared, and stationed themselves between the coming danger and their fat master – and right in front of the man in the dragonscale cowl. He had no doubt now. The cringing Cattlesmith Cal knew what was coming and his fear was worse than his confidence coming in.

The real reason the man in the dragon scale cowl was locked in here was coming.

And he was ready.

Or so he thought.

From the wall behind Zetra a purple-scaled snake women darted out. A night lamia.

Her upper half a beautiful women in a black serpent scaled corset, the lower half a snake, in a black whorish short and tight skirt, and her tail was all purple scaled with plenty of gleaming poisoned spikes.

The night lamia had coiled herself around Zetra before any of the lycan could react.

Squeezed tight.

Hissed, "Tasty."

"Not yet," said a gruff man's voice down the hall just as the owner of the voice stepped into view.

The speaker was a massive crimson iron skeleton. He was dressed in a brown long coat and slacks and thick boots. Thumping in his chest was a massive exposed heart, but exposing such a weakness, when it comes to magic, meant this skeleton was *tough*. Weakness came in hand with strength in this world and the man in the dragon scale cowl didn't want to live in one without such a fair exchange.

This skeleton had a pair of broadsword rifles was on its back, and its ribs doubled as countless curved scimitars. Its hands were claws more razor sharp and powerful than the wolfmen's.

The man in the dragon scale cowl knew this creature: a crimson skeletist.

And it needed fresh human skeletons and the souls of their prior owners to persist in this world. If not, it would cease to exist in a very painful way, and hitting its heart would kill it but that was far easier said than done.

"My ssssister needsssss fresh meat, Kilgore," the night lamia said, "And thissss vixen issss the gift that can keep giving."

Vixen did have remarkable regeneration and that, along

with how delicious their flesh was to their fellow monsters, all in all, it made them precious prey.

Claw and Fang were already snarling silently.

So it wasn't a damsel in distress honey pot trap.

The crimson skeletist Kilgore grumbled. "Not so fast, Nixie."

The wolves didn't dare leave the big and frightened Cattlesmith Cal unprotected from the newcomers. They blocked him off in that narrows passage before the bars.

"Now wait a moment there, Miss," Cattlesmith Cal said, "My vixen is –"

That night lamia Nixie hissed. "You wisssh to take her plasssssse?"

"No no no no no," Cattlesmith Cal said, "That ain't what–"

Kilgore drew one of his scimitar ribs and slashed the throat of Fang.

"We need live flesh," Kilgore said, "And this one prisoner ain't enough."

"The others?" the man in the dragon scale cowl said.

"Where you'd think," Kilgore said and his skeletal grin seemed to widen somehow.

But the man in the dragon scale cowl merely stood firm, behind the bars, trusting his dragon scale to protect him from the coming sudden unseen strike, so better stand tall and ready to react.

But he knew better than to think of how he should react.

Not with mindreaders like Zetra around.

Nixie broke the moment with a hiss.

"Sssssomething'sss wrong withhhhh that one," she said.

She coiled tight around Zetra so hard she gasped and crunches came within her. Bones breaking but lycan like her have regeneration. It wouldn't kill her unless she ran out of stamina but slow strangulation could drain her stamina till dead and a bad death at that.

Yet Zetra managed to gasp. Whimper.

"He's just ... a ... passer ... byer ..." Zetra said, "Nothing ... more ..."

With that the man in the dragon scale cowl knew whose side she was on and saving her wouldn't be easy. Not with his Code of a True Man and that night lamia Nixie was a women, of sorts, and a vile evil women at that, he wouldn't kill her but how to defeat her ...

"I'm a gravestone mason," he said, "And I heard there was some work here in this town."

It was part truth too. Some time ago he had begun training as such. Long time ago. He made journeyman before ... his new life begun. For now, he just trusted he would do so when the time was right, but the time wasn't right yet. The air was chillier than that sky high mountain pass he crossed in the dead of night to get here, and it wasn't all entirely from how cold the air was.

Like bad memories best not remembered.

"Thissss vixen can't control her powersssss," Nixie said, "Asss I thought, but her potential ... yesssss, she will nissssssely. We can revive the dragon prinsssessss tonight. The sssserpent moon aready rissses. Your zombie dragon shall–"

"Careful wench," Kilgore said, "My dragon friend don't take kindly to orders."

"You mean mount," Nixie said, "Not even a dragon friend–"

Kilgore drew one of his broadsword rifles quicker than a rattler strike. Aimed it straight at the side of Nixie's head.

No, tapped the razor point against her pointy ear. If her pale skin weren't truly protective scale, she would of lost that ear. Her twisted expression, no hiding how much that jab pained her body and ego.

"Golda!" Kilgore said, "Now!"

The wall behind the, twisted and cracked and molded itself into ... the side of a gray dragon. Its eyes ... just gaps where eyes should of been. The stink ... of a corpse long rotted and musty. The source of that hint of blood was now more than just a hint. The gray scales ... whatever color in life it had were lost in its revival from death and between its countless spikes over its head and head a familiar hole between its mean eye sockets ...

Eye sockets that suddenly turned toward the man in the dragon scale cowl.

A deep foul breath as cold as death itself ...

"*Him!*" Golda said, "He is ... the wretch who slew me!"

"And will slay you again," the man in the dragon scale cowl said and embraced the moment he had been waiting for.

The reason he avoided mindreading so carefully.

Quicker than gun shot, the man summoned his five scimitars of death. Like a sun of steel rays blazing around him. Him, the Drake Dragon Slayer of the Steel Sun.

All five blades sliced through the bars.

Destroyed the zombie dragon's head.

Kill her for the last time. The final time. For a female dragon, not a women, so it wasn't against the code.

"A flower for zee departed," Zetra said, "Rose Coffin!"

All around the vixen witch a rose of ice bloomed instant. Engulfed the night lamia like a coffin of ice in the form of a rose.

"Dust to zee dust," Zetra said and stretched sexy, with a sly smirk.

Shattering the rose coffin.

And the night lamia.

Both shattering into ... dust.

"Don't move!" Kilgore said.

He already had both broadsword rifles out and aimed. At Zetra and Drake.

BANG!

A shot rang out and it wasn't from any rifle.

Cattlesmith Cal had drawn a hidden revolver. Shot Kilgore in the heart. The crimson skeletist gasped. Howled.

"Vixen," Kilgore said, "Grant me a second life with your Abyssmal gem! I order you!"

The crimson skeletist reached for that odd gem, but the moment he touched it, Zetra froze herself from the gem inward in a rose coffin and froze Kilgore's arms. Shattered herself. Her remains falling backwards. His frozen arms now held the Abyssmal gem but in a rose coffin of ice.

Drake dashed out of the gap his scimitars had made in the bars.

"Blast you human!" Kilgore said and tried shifting his arms.

The ice engulfing his arms cracked – but didn't budge.

They couldn't block the five scimitars Jace drove into the crimson skeletist's heart. Destroying it.

Another howl and Kilgore shattered into dust.

A whimper came from behind Drake. He turned. On the ground ... Zetra. Recovered due to her regeneration, but bare in the fur now. Jace didn't hesitate to offer his hand to the young furry lass and she didn't hesitate to take it.

"Now that, my dear Zetra," Cattlesmith Cal said, "Is what the dark is truly like."

Click! Her collar fell off?

Yet the shock and horror suddenly in her eyes ... like a long lost ghost haunting her ...

"Father," she said, "I ... zank you, but ... I ..."

"Your brothers are still determined to join the dark," he said, "No helping them."

"But my poor little sister," she said, "Jacculus Jack using her ... my promise to her ..."

"Leave Fang and Claw to me," Cattlesmith Cal said, "And that dragon bastard–"

"May I ... help zee man in the dragon scale cowl?" she said, "His code ... in return ... maybe ... help against Jacculus Jack and ..."

"If that's what he asks for ..." Cattlesmith Cal said, "But a grown single women like you traveling alone with a man ... I don't like it, and few men of any sort would go up against Jacculus Jack for any reason."

"Better zan traveling alone veethout a man," she said, "If ... he agrees ... even if ..."

They all looked at Drake.

And Drake ... grimaced, sighed and ... gave Zetra another look over and ... sigh ... and nodded.

"Could use someone to watch my back," he said, "And I never met a finer woman willing to fight a serpent. Or a crimson skeletist."

Zetra stepped over. Shifted back to her stunningly gorgeous elf girl form.

"Traveling not as your sister," she said, "But as your wife ... since you never met a finer woman ... we all know the oaths ..."

Drake couldn't stop his heart from racing ... he didn't expect this but ... a guy needed to know when to take a chance or lose it forever.

"I do," he said, "And we'll kill Jacculus Jack dead and rescue that sister of yours."

She smooched him juicy soft?

It's been so long since he felt such a sensation ...

And he kissed his new wife back.

# A War Of Lust And Oak

## Read Now!

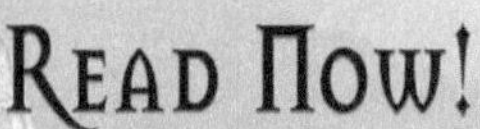

# The Elf Girl Effect

## Read Now!

The acclaimed Jonathan Evan Hudson once again weaves an unforgettable tale brimming with spicy page-turning action and fast-burning enemies-to-lovers passion.

Meet the newly knighted Roo Vorshaya. Sworn to protect humanity in the isolated mountain town of Appleharth. Dreams of action-packed adventure and passionate love under a lovely but sinister strawberry-pink sky.

Love re-ignited by a whiff of the familiar peaches and cream scent of his long-lost childhood girlfriend: the notorious elven witch Amber Peaches.

And endangering everything Roo holds dear.

Love page-turner novels of epic fantasy? Love reading from dusk to dawn? Then go read *The Elf Girl Effect* now!

# Martial Art Of The Phantom Saber

## Read Now!

# Succubus Slash

The acclaimed Jonathan Evan Hudson weaves an unforgettable tale of thrilling action and adventure spiced with fast-burning romance and doused deep in epic fantasy.

Enter Miles Mayhem. Rich in friends and enemies. And a fat boy badass in the sword.

A seriously delicious smell of bacon and eggs smothered in spiced razor-hot cheddar signals celebration—and serious trouble ahead.

Trouble beyond anything Miles ever expected.

The perfect epic fantasy novel. A genre-enlarging feast for fans of sexy action and fabulous adventure. Read *Succubus Slash* now!

# Sword Master Of Honey Heart Resort

## Read Now!

# Into Shadow Forest

## Read Now!

A diamond in the rough the bestselling Jonathan Evan Hudson weaves a thrilling tale from explosive beginning to satisfying end in the awe-inspiring land of Grandcrest.

The talented twenty-something sword master Romeo Bladell yearns for love and adventure.

And at the musty edges of Shadow Forest. Near the towering high oaks bearded like stout old dwarves. By a canyon like a wound gnashed deep through in the granite. A canyon like the maw of a stone dragon.

A strange unexpected rope bridge hangs silently. Sinisterly.

Beckoning adventure—and danger unimaginable.

Enter *Into Shadow Forest* and savor the most spectacular of page-turning epic fantasy novels. Love unique monsters, riveting battles, and fantastic femme fatales? Then read *Into Shadow Forest* now!

# Angels Of The Sword

## Read Now!

# Crossing Of Shadowed Death

## Read Now!

The acclaimed master of fantasy Jonathan Evan Hudson once again shines through with his talented story-telling. Time to enter another stunning awe-inspiring world of dangerous demons, magical mayhem, and action-packed adventure.

A simple demon-hunting mission. The young and lonely Dirk yearns for amazing adventure, for gorgeously under-dressed dancer girls among the towering high ferns. Among the even taller pines of the hot and humid Fern Shadow Forest.

Pine needles everywhere. And so fragrant they made the finest of teas.

Sturdy reliable cobble roads of the Divine Empire cut through the whole entire forest. Providing the only safe passage.

Or so Dirk thought ...

Enjoy this sexy, action-packed epic fantasy adventure from the talented Jonathan Evan Hudson. Love to read an enthralling epic fantasy novel full of stunning rip-roaring battles with creative new monsters? Then go read *Crossing of Shadowed Death* now!

# A TASTE OF THE ELF GIRL EFFECT

*The acclaimed Jonathan Evan Hudson once again weaves an unforgettable tale brimming with spicy page-turning action and fast-burning enemies-to-lovers passion.*

*Meet the newly knighted Roo Vorshaya. Sworn to protect humanity in the isolated mountain town of Appleharth. Dreams of action-packed adventure and passionate love under a lovely but sinister strawberry-pink sky.*

*Love re-ignited by a whiff of the familiar peaches and cream scent of his long-lost childhood girlfriend: the notorious elven witch Amber Peaches.*

*And endangering everything Roo holds dear.*

*Love page-turner novels of epic fantasy? Love reading from dusk to dawn? Then go read **The Elf Girl Effect** now!*

# CHAPTER 1
## R⌀⌀

The sky was a strawberry custard for the eyes, and the same color of the lips Roo yearned to kiss.

So what if the clouds behind him were dark and ominous? The wind gusty and chilled more than the perfect shot of vodka. The taste of rain electrified by lightning-to-be ...

The street was as slim as his chances of success.

The cobble as bumpy as the journey ahead.

And this hill — a steep ascent into danger.

Roo even wore a jerkin woven of the finest dragon scale the son of ~~an~~ thee Exiled Exorcist of Most Notable Notoriety could hope to earn as one of the last members of the Vorshaya Clan.

Yup.

The Vorshaya clan. The once very badassed clan nearly wiped out to protect the greatest of the great Oak of Ages, a source of lightful magic and all from ... something, something he'd hunt down and deal with.

Still, if his mother hadn't been doing scholarly stuff far away at the time ... if she hadn't taken him with her ...

Sigh.

He didn't like to think about it much.

But his jerkin was pale blue as the sky ... wasn't today.

But it was one only worn by the best of the best True TriCross Knights. The big, white triple cross on his chest proclaimed it for all to see.

And a chance to pursue his dream to travel the world.

Slay monsters and save people, without any of that bounty hunter nonsense either.

Explores things, places that no one's ever explored before, or okay, more like no one's explored in living memory ...

Or longer.

His jerkin, it even had the snazziest, puffiest shoulder guards of the palest, bluest cold silver, and they were so so perfectly round that a certain Motherly Scholar of Notable Nagging couldn't hope to find a single fault with.

Just like the trusty pouch she made for him.

Shaped like a chubby triple cross, it was strapped to his waist and she magicked it to hold far more than you'd think it could and weigh so much less.

And just like his pouch, his slacks were as blue as the sky ... wasn't ... today.

And ... okay okay.

Anyways, his boots, and girls were obsessed with footwear or else the boot merchants wouldn't cater to girls so utterly much, so anyways, his boots were a snazzy dark blue suede, like the coming night sky should be (but obviously won't be. Pink sky meant severe storm coming.)

And with the coming storm ...

There were even spooky tentacles of mist rising from the street, and that only happened when a serious storm was coming through.

But the not so distant rumbles ... wasn't only thunder.

So not much time left ...

Good thing he wore a pair of sabers and a whip. One saber was of the bluest, sharpest cold silver, and the other, the blackest, sharpest cold steel, a stronger variant of cold iron, and the whip was made of pretty strong scarlet dragon scales, with the dragon magic woven strongly within the whip.

Good for offense and defense, against magical and nonmagical trouble too.

Sort of.

As long as he didn't whip his eye out, like his mother often teased.

Even more important, his trusty arm guards were both cold silver and cold steel forged together. His left arm guard could extend into a shield. The right held a miniature bow with a string of holy blue magic so that, with the right motion flicking motion, it would fire bolts of holy blue light or unholy violet light.

Perfect for a True TriCross Knight.

His heart raced for the coming battle.

For the girl she would soon save.

Since nothing, absolutely *nothing* raced a heart like that

elven fragrance, that whiff of the sweetest of peaches and cream only moments ago in this sweet sweltering hot afternoon.

No doubt about it.

The elf girl of his wildest dream come true. Right now. Here in the sexy flesh ...

Amber Peaches: a lust dream come true.

No.

*Thee* one and **best** lust dream come true.

And the muddy road here was a nice reminder of years ago, back when Peaches and Row got to quipping each other and their quipping got so fierce it broke out into mud wrestling that if, today their reunion broke into mud wrestling, wow, that would be so sexy amazing ...

Sniiiiiiiff.

It smelled ... surprisingly fresh. Earthy forest mud, no, soil fresh.

The lampposts at the street corners ... they were cold iron. The blackest of cold iron and forged like incredibly narrow, but tall, tulips of utter moonless midnight black.

Ah.

The oil lamps on top were those genie-style lamps to be wicked for the evening and wow, did they make the olive oil merchants rich.

But ... it was the genies inside that kept the mud clean. Kept their lamps lit at night, but what those genies were ...

Elf girls captured and lamped into genies due to the war between humans and demons, and well, elves were demons after all, and elves were the fully evolved form of fairies.

Even Peaches.

But the rumble of distant thunder that wasn't thunder was almost louder than his own tummy rumbling for some peaches and cream pie, especially after that sexy whiff of long missed Peaches.

(All better to tease Peaches with too.)

((Sure, elves should thank the Light their natural body odor, after lots of sweaty work, was so fruity nice rather than so gut-wrenching stinky like humans, you know, like him, but either way, frequenting the public baths, a necessity, human or elf.))

(But not first date material.)

((Outside of certain smut rags kept hidden under the best lock and key in an undisclosed location.))

(((*Very* undisclosed.)))

Even now, the sun was still as blonde as Peaches' waist-long hair, so no worries.

Last they ran into each other, back before war and puberty tore them apart, her hair was ass-long but also far far messier.

Just like back then, she styled the bangs to fountain off the sides of her head like gorgeously floppy wings, plus a floppy witch hat of rosy pink, that, of course, would hide her huuuuge but adorably pointy elf ears.

Ears so long and pointy, that resembled a cross between kitty and fawn ears, especially how they always were moving about so expressively.

So all in all, he wasn't so distracted by her fine ass in a finer minidress, (and it was the ultra-short, ultra snug and stretchy kind that was like strawberry custard to the eyes, ears, and loins,) so no, in that critical moment, he didn't walk into a wall.

No.

He walked into a door.

And as the Light would have it, there was plenty of wall he could of walked into.

The stone floors of the half-timber houses all along this block. All painted as colorfully as a field of wildflowers, but full of apples, apple blossoms, and even more apples.

This town was called Appleharth for a reason.

A very good reason.

And the door he did walk into was the usual solid sturdy oak, so no worries, it took the beating well.

Sure, there was ... a crack down the middle of the door now.

Sure. From him.

But the door's paint job was still spectacular.

No clumsy clod could hope to ruin those artful swathes of banana streaks full of cherry swirls. In fact, there wasn't even a nick to show for his clumsy moment.

Other than a wide crack down the middle.

And by the hinges too.

Roo credited his snazzy cowl and mouth cloth for softening the blow. They were as pale blue as the sky ... wasn't ... today.

But they were the color of Peaches' bright blue eyes ... well, last time they ran into each other years and years ago, over a decade ago. More than a decade ago. Wait. Same thing. Okay.

Good.

Dazed but not confused. A door would not stop him.

Or delay him.

Much.

Now one more chance or else ... he'd regret it for the rest of his life.

# CHAPTER 2
# PEACHES

Totally fucking ... that poster of parchment ... those blocky black letters spelling WANTED ...

Oh, for the Oak of Ages ... Peaches totally fucking wanted to give the middle finger to that sly sneak of a trickster the moment she spotted that parchment poster hanging all cozy and sinister and sooo much like a little black widow on those shutters behind the windowsill of those stinkier than stinky roses.

The sky wouldn't be the only one growling soon.

Good thing Peaches wore her finger loop gloves snug and ready. Each was as scarlet red as she'd soon make that trickster, what's her face, the Rouge Reapist, and even better, there were pentacles of unicorn hair woven into each palm to speed up her magic casting faster than a fox pouncing a mouse.

Along the glove were cute heart-shaped gaps. Normally, they'd hold rosy pink hearts, each of which held a precast spell she could fling at a target for instant effect, but she ran out a while ago and seeing a human alchemist ... pretty dangerous when her kind made such good ingredients to those sorts.

But that thunder close by, not just thunder.

The narrow street echoed the rumble and only confirmed the groan of a dire ogre coming this way.

Strange how there weren't any screams.

Disturbing, in fact.

Regular people shouldn't be so calm around one, unless ... no.

Peaches didn't want to think of it.

Yet.

It was bad enough that the pink sky, as lovely as it was, meant the coming storm would be terrible, if her father's stories held any truth to them.

(Big if.)

But no telling what these half-timber houses were hiding then. So what if they were beautifully decorated with apples, apples, and more apples? Plus a flower or two.

A chill seemed to ache her whole spine.

A warning of danger.

Demonic danger.

Nearby.

Never mind elves were technically lightspawn, a kind of demon, but of the light, so too many humans, sigh.

Least she usually could be reborn a few more times.

More than a few, actually.

Nine lives, like a cat, but three already used, but least her power and beauty were upped each time, but she started out as a brand new fairy, hatching from the Oak of Ages, and had to find another compatible human girl to fuse with, eat her soul and sigh.

No wonder some human despised demons of   all sorts.

If her brother only had one life ... if she only had one life ... like these humans ... sigh.

Why Roo even understood way back when ... sigh.

But the lamppost of black iron, horribly styled like tall and narrow tulips, no, that burn to their smell, a burn like that death pepper chili that little brat Roo tricked her stupid bratty self into trying long ago (and stupid her tried it again and again and again ...)

But it was definitely cold iron.

A quick way to a really, really awful death.

No wonder she couldn't pinpoint the source of demonic danger.

No doubt it was darkspawn demons but so what?

This was just a step toward her true dream, becoming an elf witch explorer, and discover why there's so many ruins appearing here and there, and elves had extension records proving some of these ruins appeared without a civilization before, as if it had been moved there.

Some even came from the future.

Others were from the distant past. Ruins that should no longer exist.

Ruins full of monsters.

So today, good practice.

Peaches made a point to keep strutting down the road without hesitation or obvious concern.

If orcs were hunting her ... letting them know she sensed something suspicious, especially as a witch with her foresense able to detect danger and ill intent toward her, well, according to her training, a big no no.

And despite it being in the early afternoon, the shutters of all the half-timber houses were shut.

Locked.

Other human towns she'd been in ... plenty of dumb human girls overlooked her demonic side and drooled over her looks, but here, today? Nope. Not one dumbass to brush off.

Something was off.

Good thing she could summon her bow and arrows of light quicker than any other elf in her generation, guy or girl. Several split seconds ahead of the best of the best guys and rapid fire better too. She could even build up plenty of blessed arrows as long as she got enough sunlight during the day, each day to build up and store more blessings for arrows for when she'd need them.

At least if any orc managed to get too close, the stiletto heels of her thigh boots could double as slyly placed daggers.

Alicorn style. Beauty and power came together for elf girls, so lucky her.

And her alicorn was the high grade spiraled kind.

Her boots were as scarlet red as she'd made those orcs.

Normally, she had rosy pink hearts lacing them snug up her leg. They normally would hold spells she could fling off for instant magical attacks just like her gloves.

But right now, like her gloves, they were just a bunch of heart-shaped gaps.

At least her rosy pink minidress and witch hat were woven with silk of a spellbinder silkworm. They weren't protective against blade and fang, or even against magic ... but they both together were a huge reserve of extra magic that naturally refilled as long as she wore them enough, especially in sunlight.

Even today.

And to fuck with the mind of those perverted orc bastards, she went with the sluttiest minidress she could manage. Translucent silk, so the right angles, the right nude elf deluxe, he-he.

So double the weirdness that no human guys went lusty dumbass toward her today.

Not even the gate guards.

Okay. Gate guards rarely did. Being a guard was all reputation and honor, not about coin. Any act tarnishing that, tarnished all the guards, and the guard loathed that.

Plus, her rosy pink minidress had the perfect distract and destroy notch down the front. One that showed far more than the little it covered.

Including her bra of ruby hearts.

And her chest, buxom to the extreme.

With only a few stretched to the breaking ruby ties down each the notches, the slutty side notches revealed more than just her tasty midriff, they revealed a good solid hint of her lace panties.

Ruby lace.

Orcs were rapeholic monsters, after all. She might as well use their lust smitten idiocy against them.

Roo would so laugh and approve.

(And leer.)

((Leer plenty.))

(((Sigh. *Boys*.)))

((((But if he didn't ... her pointy tipped boots, his rear, he-he.))))

# WANT MORE?

Go to

# WANT MORE?

Go to

www.JonathanEvanHudson.com